Sox Looks for Home

(Sox's Pawtograph)

I enthusiastically dedicate this book to:

SOX, our mischievous, wonderful orange tabby cat. His three real-life runaway adventures inspired me to write this story.

My wife **SUE**, who introduced me to the unique world of cats over 50 years ago. Our anguish over Sox's runs added a memorable chapter to our marriage.

ZOLA (then 11), **GEORGIE** (then 8) and **CLAIRE** (then 7), my first "focus group" of children. Their helpful insights encouraged me to improve Sox's story in important ways.

I also offer special thanks to **JULIE COYLE**, a very talented illustrator whose whimsical art and writing skills guided me through the maze of book publishing. Additionally, Julie is simply a very delightful person.

ISBN: 978-1-0879-6801-8

Published in association with:
Keokee Co. Publishing, Inc.
Sandpoint, Idaho
www.keokeebooks.com

Sox Looks for Home

written by Paul Graves   Illustrated by Julie Coyle

Sox sat beside Pepper.
Together, they watched birds flying in the cage on
the floor of the Kitty Hotel in the Pet Hospital.

Pepper chattered at the birds, then said...
"I think those birds would fly right out of this
room if they could. Birds should be free."

Sox looked at Pepper, "Yes, they would.
I know I got away when I could."

"What do you mean?" Pepper asked.

3

"Not long ago, my people brought me here. When they picked me up, they took me to a house I'd never seen before.

4

Different smells.

Different feels.

Different everything. Yuck!

After some days inside, they let me out...

And I began to sniff my way back to my old home.

I jumped.

SQUEEK!

I scrambled.

and made it across the highway into the woods.

7

I looked

and looked for my home.

It took a few days, but eventually I made it.

8

My feet hurt.   I was hungry.   But I was home.

Or at least I thought so. Two smelly dogs
lived there now, and no one would let me in.

9

Some days later, my people found me in the alley behind the old house. They gave me food. I was very hungry, and while I was eating they picked me up.

Then I was back in the new house with the strange smells. But the food was good. And I really enjoyed their attention."

... but I had to run up a tree twice to escape barking dogs.

HEY, LOOK! ANOTHER CAT!

WE SHOULD CHASE IT!

I also ran away from a skunk

and saw a raccoon digging through a trash can.

13

As I got to the old home again, big,
cold winds started to blow.

Those smelly dogs were still there and no one
would let me in, so I curled up in a shed.

My people came looking for me every day.
But I was afraid they would take me back to the strange house,
so I hid from them.

I found food on the porch at my old house and at the house on the other side of the fence.

16

I saw an orange cat, like me, in the window of each house!

One day, the man came close to the shed and called my name.

Sox?

MEOW! MEOW!

I called back.

He brought me food, and I was very hungry. While I was eating, he picked me up and put me in my carrier.

TUNA

I didn't mind."

Pepper had never wanted to stray from her own home, so she was happy that Sox had been brought back.

"And you stayed home this time?" She asked.

"I wasn't let out of the new house for a long time.

18

The smells weren't as strange this time, but the old home smells were still in my nose.

The lady would let me out when she was also outside. After a while, they thought I would stay around.

19

But one night when I was let outside I ran away again.
It took three days to find my way to the old home this time.

I made it across
the highway

and I went around the
barking dogs,

and steered clear of
the skunk.

But one grumpy person
chased me off his lawn,

and another man
tried to pick me up.

STAY OFF GRASS!

20

At night I stayed still in the shadows away from street lights, afraid other cats or dogs would see me.

Finally, I found my way back to my old house. Those smelly dogs were still there and no one would let me in!"

"You got away a third time?" Pepper asked. "You must really miss that house."

"I guess I did," Sox said, "but it was different this time.

I was really lonely for my people, but it was like I couldn't find my way back to the strange house. So, I hung out where I was, until my people came looking for me again.

Sox?

I had gotten kinda wild by that time. I was afraid to be close to them, even when they brought me food.

I scratched at the lady.

I ran from the man.

ZOOM!

23

I was afraid and wanted to be left alone.

But there was food at the two houses I told you about, so I stayed close by.

One day, I saw food in a dish that sat inside a wire box.

I was hungry so I slowly crept in, and as I took a bite...

BANG!

...a wire door came down
hard and kept me inside".

"What happened to you?" Pepper asked.
"How did you get out?"

25

"Soon, the man came and picked up the box I was in.

"YEOWL!"

I was so angry and scared.
I scratched at the wire.
I hissed and screamed.

Soon I was in the car and going back to the new house.

When we got inside, the man put the wire box down and opened the door for me. This time, I had a different feeling in the new house. I felt calmer. I felt happy and safe.

27

My people have kept me inside since. It was cold and wintry outside.

I hope the weather gets better soon so I can go back outside again".

Pepper asked,
"Will you go back to your old house?"

Sox turned to Pepper with a little smile and responded,

"I might. The old house was home for so long.

But my people love me and treat me so well in the new house.

Lots of lap-sitting,
soft chin strokes,

lying on the window sill in
the warm sun,

the food bowl and water dish
always full.

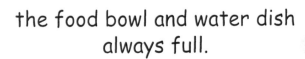

So, I might stick around with them.

All I want is to be home."

Sox looked at the cage and chattered at the birds.

31

BIOGRAPHIES

PAUL GRAVES

Author Paul Graves is a retired and re-focused United Methodist pastor and geriatric social worker. He also has written a faith-and-values column for the Spokesman-Review for over 25 years, as well as a 12-year column on aging issues, "Dear Geezer." This children's story is his first book. Paul lives in Sandpoint, Idaho, with his wife, Sue, and their cat, Sox. Contact Paul at elderadvocates@nctv.com

SOX

Sox is a 6-year-old orange tabby cat with an adventurous spirit. His story is based on his three real-life run-aways to his old home. At least 5 of his 9 lives were expended during these adventures!

JULIE COYLE

Illustrator Julie Coyle holds an MFA in creative writing for children from Spalding University and a graduate certificate in children's book illustration from Hollins University. Much of her work is inspired by the cast of zany animals that she's been honored to have as pets. She currently lives in Pullman, Washington, with her awesome husband, two amazing step-kids, one anxious (but lovable) dog, two fluffy bunnies, and a handful of squawky chickens. Visit her at juliecoyle.com.

CPSIA information can be obtained
at www.ICGtesting.com
Printed in the USA
BVRC101059170821
614616BV00004B/46

9781087968018